For Isolde and Oscar, my little monsters - K.E.

For my good friend Freda - S.M.

First published in Great Britain in 2004 by
Frances Lincoln Children's Books, 4 Torriano Mews,
Torriano Avenue, London NW5 2RZ
www.franceslincoln.com

British Library Cataloguing in Publication Data
available on request

ISBN 1-84507-067-4

Set in Wunderlich Medium and Copperplate

Printed in Singapore
1 3 5 7 9 8 6 4 2

MYTHS
AND
MONSTERS

Katie Edwards • Illustrated by Simon Mendez

FRANCES LINCOLN CHILDREN'S BOOKS

CONTENTS

INTRODUCTION

Myths are stories which are partly true, but also partly made up to sound more frightening or fantastic.

Hundreds of years ago, many of the animals we are familiar with today, such as rhinoceroses, antelopes and elephants, were unknown to the western world. Only a few brave explorers ventured into new lands, often catching glimpses of strange, new creatures on their travels – and when something looks strange, it can seem scary and threatening.

Early explorers also discovered mysterious remains and tried to explain what they were. Scientists did not yet know that, long before human beings evolved, whole groups of extraordinary animals had lived, died and become extinct, leaving only their fossils behind. So when, for example, explorers found fossilised sharks' teeth, they believed them to be tongues that had fallen from the sky and turned to stone during an eclipse of the moon. Ammonites, an extinct relative of squid, were once known as "snake stones" and thought to be coiled, headless snakes. Fossilised sea urchins were highly prized as magical snake eggs long ago.

So the travellers returned home with tales of the fabulous beasts they had found. And, rather like a game of Chinese Whispers, as their stories were told over and over again by different people, details often got changed or exaggerated during the telling.

In the following pages you can read the stories of ten legendary creatures and discover the reality behind the myths.

ROC

A **YOUNG MAN**
called Sindbad, hungry for adventure,
joined some sea-merchants setting sail across
the Indian Ocean. On his second voyage he
found himself stranded on a lush tropical island.

As he explored, he came across an enormous white
egg. It was so large that it took Sindbad 50 paces to walk
around it! Suddenly the sky went dark. As Sindbad looked up,
a gigantic white bird, a bit like an eagle or albatross, flew down
and landed beside the egg.

Sindbad had heard tales of this amazing bird, known as a Roc,
from sailors, and he decided to strap himself on to one of its massive
legs and escape from the island. The next day the Roc flew off, carrying
Sindbad with it. When at last it landed in a deep valley, Sindbad untied
himself and continued on his travels.

We now know that stories of the Roc are probably based on an extinct
giant bird. It was nicknamed "the elephant bird" by Marco Polo,
an Italian explorer who travelled across Asia about 800 years ago.
The elephant bird died out over 300 years ago, but its fossilised
remains reveal that it was the biggest bird that ever lived. At 3 metres,
it was so tall that if it were alive today, it would be able to peer into
the top of a double-decker bus. It laid eggs as long as your arm!
Although the Roc that Sindbad met could fly, the real elephant
bird could not, and so was confined to its home of Madagascar,
a rich tropical island off the east coast of Africa.

LAKE MONSTER

DEEP, MURKY LAKES are just as popular as the open ocean for inspiring tales of underwater monsters.

Nessie, perhaps the world's most famous lake monster, is believed to live in Loch Ness, in Scotland. The biggest lake in the United Kingdom, it is also very long, extremely deep and contains peat, which turns the water a murky brown. Viking sagas were the first to mention an elusive lake monster, but during the last 70 years there have been many reported sightings of a hump-backed creature in Loch Ness. Photographs have been produced as evidence, but they tend to be distant and out of focus.

A lake monster called Opopogo is thought to exist in Lake Okanagan, in Canada, and Mokele-Mbembe is a dinosaur-like creature believed to lurk in the swamps of Central Africa.

We now know that the most convincing photo of Nessie, known as the "Surgeon's picture", is a fake. Taken in 1934, it was created using a small model. Sonar tracking surveys over the last 30 years have also failed to reveal any large creature living in the lake. A plesiosaur that has survived from the dinosaur age is the most popular explanation for the monster – and four vertebrae believed to be from a 10.5 metre-long plesiosaur were found in 2003 on the banks of Loch Ness. But these long-necked reptiles lived in the sea, not fresh water, and to survive the last 65 million years there would need to be enough of them to form a breeding population.

However, the coelacanth is a proven example of a "living fossil". This large, deep-sea fish was thought to have been extinct for nearly 70 million years until one was caught, alive and well, in 1938.

Pythons could account for the Mokele-Mbembe sightings in the African Congo. These snakes can reach 10 metres in length and they sometimes enter the water to catch fish, but keep their heads above the water to breathe.

CYCLOPS (meaning "round eye")

was the name given to the one-eyed, man-eating giant of Greek mythology. This ancient race of wild, lawless ogres was thought to have been shaped from fire and rock.

The Greek king Odysseus was curious to meet these creatures when his ships sailed to their island. He was hiding in a cave when a Cyclops called Polyphemus entered with his flock of rams. Seeing the invaders, Polyphemus sealed the cave entrance, seized a few sailors, devoured them alive and settled down to sleep.

Trapped in the cave, Odysseus sharpened a red-hot stake and plunged it into Polyphemus' single huge eye. The ogre bellowed with pain as his eye hissed and sizzled. The next morning, Odysseus and the remaining sailors escaped and sailed away under a shower of rocks hurled from the cliffs by the blinded Cyclops.

CYCLOPS

We now know that the Greeks discovered large fossil bones and teeth in caves on Mediterranean islands, which probably fuelled their belief in giants. The large central hole in some of the skulls was thought to be the single eye-socket of a Cyclops.

The Cyclops myth was believed until just over 100 years ago, when a French scientist called Georges Cuvier compared the fossil bones of the "giants" with the bones of living animals. He realised that skulls with a large central hole belonged to elephants and that the hole indicated the position of the elephant's trunk.

An adventurous English lady called Dorothea Bate travelled alone to Cyprus in 1901. She unearthed many fossils and concluded that dwarf elephants and hippopotamuses roamed the island until about 10,000 years ago.

THE NAME "CHIMERA"

means an imaginary beast made from parts of different animals. According to Ancient Greek legend, the Chimera was a fire-breathing, female monster with a lion's head, a goat's body and a snake's tail. When she attacked local people in the mountains of Lycia (now part of Turkey), the king offered a reward for killing her. A boy called Bellerophon took up the challenge, and riding the winged horse Pegasus, hunted down and killed the beast.

Other legendary chimeras include the Griffin, which is half-eagle, half-lion; the Centaur – half-human, half-horse; and the Minotaur – half-human, half-bull.

CHIMERA

We now know that despite all the myths, chimeras have never existed. The first dried skin of a platypus, an Australian egg-laying mammal, was sent to Britain over 200 years ago. People thought it was some kind of chimera, suggesting it was created by attaching a duck's beak to the body of a mammal.

Recent scientific advances in genetic technology have given scope for creating modern-day chimeras in the laboratory, such as the "geep", formed from a sheep and a goat, and the "cama", which has a llama mother and a camel father. Technology has also triggered experiments in some of our food and medicines. Genes from the ice-fish have been used to breed frost-resistant tomatoes. And insulin, which was originally removed from the pancreas of slaughtered pigs and cattle to treat diabetes, is now produced from genetically-modified bacteria.

MERMAID

MERMAIDS, with their female heads and bodies ending in a fish's scaly tail, are often shown sitting on rocks, half out of the water, singing sweet songs. They are first mentioned in Ancient Greek mythology, and stories about them continued to be popular throughout the Middle Ages. Sightings continued until the 17th century.

Some legends tell how sailors, mesmerised by the mermaids' beautiful voices, tried to follow them to their underwater paradise, only to be lured to their death. Other tales describe kind mermaids warning sailors of sea-storms to come, bringing up deep sea treasure for them or granting their wishes.

We now know that when sailors caught sight of mermaids, they were probably seeing dugongs, manatees or seals. These animals are mammals, like us. They have adapted to life underwater, but still need to come up to the surface to breathe air.

Dugongs and manatees are huge, streamlined creatures with paddle-like flippers, no legs and a flattened tail. They swim slowly and gracefully through shallow tropical waters, grazing on sea-grasses, which is why they are also known as "sea-cows". Dugongs live around the coast of northern Australia, while manatees are found in the West Indies, West Africa and the Amazon Basin.

Seals live in colder waters, but they also bask on rocks. From a distance, their postures and cries can seem human. Fleeting glimpses of these shy creatures through mist, sea-spray or cloudy water are likely to have perpetuated the haunting myth of "the maidens of the sea".

THE HYDRA of Ancient Greek legend lived in coastal swamps. It had nine heads: the main head lived for ever and the other eight re-grew if they were cut off. The hero Hercules was commanded to kill the monster. He succeeded by smothering the Hydra's main head with a massive stone while setting fire to the other heads.

The Kraken was a Norwegian horned sea monster whose streaming tentacles were lined with jagged suckers. Sailors were afraid to disturb a sleeping Kraken, believing it would swallow their ship whole and ooze black liquid if they fought it.

Tales have also been told of a sea serpent with a horse's head and a flaming red mane. One was said to have been washed up on the shores of Orkney, off the north coast of Scotland, in 1808. It was reported to measure 19 metres in length – almost as long as two double-decker buses.

SEA SERPENT

We now know that sightings of real, but rarely-seen sea creatures can explain many mythical sea serpents.

The giant squid is similar in many ways to descriptions of the Kraken and Hydra. It can grow up to 20 metres long and usually lives in cold, dark depths of 1,000 metres or more. Little is known about these reclusive giants, but their remains have been found in the stomachs of sperm whales. From the dinner-plate-sized scars seen on sperm whales' bodies, it is thought that the giant squid lashes out with its suckered tentacles in a struggle to avoid being eaten.

The oarfish, or ribbonfish, is a flat fish that can grow up to eight metres long. It has silver skin with a scarlet fin running along its back, and might once have been mistaken for a sea serpent.

Unicorn

LEGENDS OF THE UNICORN describe a pure white,
noble, solitary creature with the powerful body of a horse and a long straight
horn jutting out from its forehead like a spear. People once believed that the horn had
magical healing properties, especially against poison.

To find the unicorn, hunters searched the depths of the darkest forests where it
was thought to live. To catch it, they took an innocent young woman into the woods.
It was believed that as soon as the unicorn saw the woman, it would run to her, lie at
her feet and rest its head on her lap. The animal would be gently stroked until it fell
asleep – only to be captured by the hunters hiding in the trees.

We now know that the idea of the unicorn may have been based on several other horned animals.

The Arabian oryx is an antelope with two slender horns which could easily have been mistaken for a single one when the animal was seen from the side.

People once thought that the single horn of the Asian rhinoceros had miraculous healing powers. These fierce animals were often trapped using a trained female monkey: the monkey would scratch the rhinoceros's back and rub its belly until it lay down, and hunters then caught it.

The extinct giant rhinoceros also had an enormous horn in the middle of its forehead. Fossils of its skull and teeth have been found in Siberia. They look rather like a horse's skull, so they may have inspired unicorn tales.

STORIES OF BLOODTHIRSTY,

fire-breathing dragons have been told in parts of Europe for over 1,000 years.

The tale of St George and the dragon is set in Libya. An evil, winged monster lurked there in a swamp, choking the countryside with its vile-smelling, poisonous breath. The king decided that the only way to stop his people from being terrorised was to sacrifice his daughter to the dragon. As she waited in terror, tied to a stake, a knight in silver armour galloped up on his horse and promised to save her. When the roaring, thrashing monster emerged from its lair, the brave knight killed it with his sword.

In ancient China, dragons were believed to be powerful, wise and magical creatures living in the sky. Their fiery breath formed the clouds and their footprints made rain fall.

DRAGON

We now know that tales of dragons in China date back 2,000 years to a time
when large fossil bones were discovered there. These bones and teeth were
often ground up and used as medicines. In 1842 the remains were correctly
identified as belonging to an extinct group of reptiles called dinosaurs,
a word that means "terrible lizards".

More recent accounts of dragons come from travellers' encounters with
giant living reptiles such as the man-eating Komodo dragon, with its thick
scaly hide, flickering tongue and poisonous bite. Found only on the islands
of Komodo and Rinca in Indonesia, it is the world's largest living lizard and
feeds on a steady supply of goats from locals and visitors.

PHOENIX

THE PHOENIX was a magnificent mythical bird with a scarlet body, blue eyes, purple feet and iridescent wings. It lived in the woods of Paradise and was said to survive on air alone.

Every 500 years, when it was time to die, the Phoenix would fly to Phoenicia, in Syria, where it made a nest from twigs, cinnamon and myrrh in the tallest palm tree. The next day, when the sun rose, its sparks would set the nest on fire. The Phoenix would open its wings and begin a graceful dance of death in the flames. As it burnt up, a new Phoenix would appear from the ashes. The new bird flew to Egypt carrying a ball of myrrh, then returned to Paradise for another 500 years.

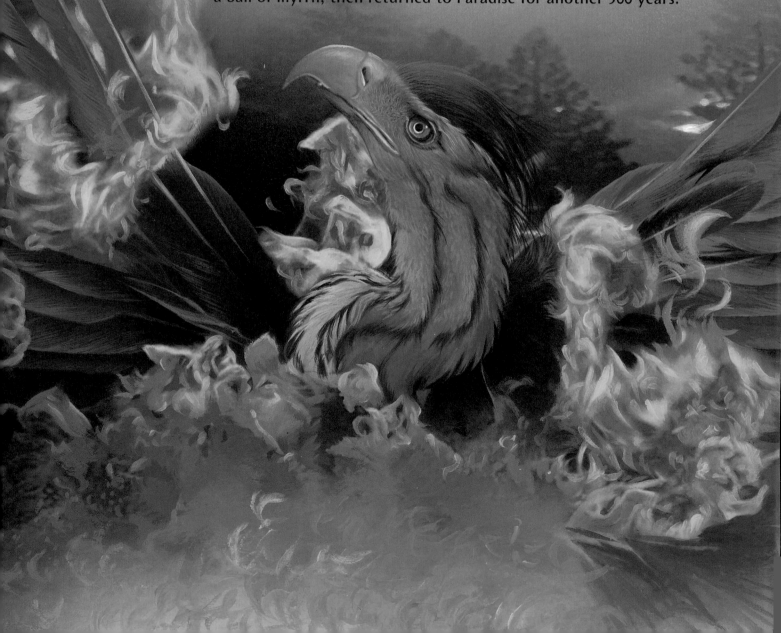

We now know that the purple heron is the closest living bird to
the Phoenix. It has purple colouring, a crest on its head and builds
its nest at the top of tall trees. In ancient Egypt, where the legend of
the sacred Phoenix began, the purple heron was worshipped as a sun-bird.
Tropical birds found in Asia – such as the golden pheasant and the bird
of paradise – have colourful feathers similar to descriptions of the Phoenix.
Early travellers and traders may have taken these birds' skins back to Egypt.
Myrrh, a sweet-smelling gum resin from trees in Africa and Asia, may have
been used to preserve the skins, so contributing to the myth.

YETI

FOR AS LONG as there have been dense forests and mountain ranges, stories have been told of wild, hairy giants lurking in them. The myth is so common that the tree-swinging apes found in the forests of Borneo and Sumatra are called orang-utans, which means "wild man of the woods".

One of the most enduring "wild man" myths is that of the Yeti, which is believed to roam the snowy slopes of the Himalayan Mountains. Local people refer to the creature's clumsy, lop-sided walk. They say that the Yeti carries a magic stone in its left armpit which is used to stun large animal prey.

From the 1920s onwards, reported sightings of the "Abominable Snowman" increased as more and more mountaineers attempted to climb Mount Everest. One account accused a Yeti of stealing chocolate bars from a tent! In the 1950s and 1960s, a photograph of a Yeti footprint and samples claimed to be the scalp and skin of a Yeti were brought back to Britain for investigation.

We now know that the Yeti footprint was probably made by a langur monkey, which often stands on two legs. Although this monkey leaves small footprints in fresh snow, if these impressions melt and re-freeze several times, they can become enlarged and distorted.

When the Yeti scalp and skin samples were taken to the Natural History Museum for identification, scientists discovered that the scalp came from a Himalayan serow goat and the skin from a blue bear. Blue bears are actually brown, and live in Tibet.

It has been suggested that the Yeti could be a distant relative of a giant ape called *Gigantopithecus*. These apes, which stood three metres tall, lived in Asia until about 300,000 years ago.

MORE ABOUT THE MYTHS AND MONSTERS

ROC

• Stories of Sindbad are told in *The Arabian Nights: Tales from a Thousand and One Nights,* a collection of ancient Arab, Persian and Indian fantasy stories.

• You can see an elephant bird egg in the *Birds* exhibition at the Natural History Museum in London.

• Hundreds of years ago, people carried water in elephant birds' discarded eggshells.

• The albatross is the largest living bird, with a wing-span of up to three metres.

LAKE MONSTER

• The famous Anglo-Saxon poem *Beowulf* describes how Beowulf kills a terrible monster called Grendel and its evil mother.

• Mary Anning was a pioneering female fossil-hunter during the early 19th century. She was the first person to discover complete fossils of plesiosaurs and ichthyosaurs on the Dorset coast, around Lyme Regis. You can see many of these graceful marine reptiles on display at the Natural History Museum.

CYCLOPS

• Odysseus' adventures are told in Homer's epic poem *The Odyssey*.

• Georges Cuvier was the founder of modern palaeontology – the study of fossils.

CHIMERA

• According to Ancient Greek legend, the Minotaur was the offspring of King Minos of Crete. Each year 14 young men and women were sacrificed to feed the beast. The hero Theseus offered to go with the victims and kill the Minotaur. Unwinding a ball of thread given to him by the Cretan king's daughter Ariadne, he found his way to the centre of the labyrinth where the Minotaur lived and killed the beast. Then he followed the thread to get out of the maze and sailed away from the island with Ariadne.

• In the 19th century, sailors moulded the dried skins of skates and rays into grotesque shapes to sell as strange beasts. People believed that these fake chimeras, known as "Jenny Hanivers", kept away evil.

MERMAIDS

• The sirens in Homer's *Odyssey* who try to lure Odysseus' boat on to the rocks with their singing were often portrayed with fishtails by Ancient Greek sculptors.

• Hans Andersen's classic story *The Little Mermaid* tells of a mermaid who, after saving a prince from drowning, falls in love with him and yearns for a human soul.

Sea Serpent

• Killing the Hydra was one of the Twelve Labours performed by the Ancient Greek hero Hercules as a punishment for killing his wife and children.

• Sea serpents are also mentioned in Homer's epic poem *The Iliad*: two great sea serpents with crimson-crested heads rush out of the sea and crush a Trojan priest and his two sons to death.

• You can see an oarfish on display at the Walter Rothschild Zoological Museum in Tring, Hertfordshire.

Unicorn

• The narwhal is a small Arctic whale with a single, long, spiralling tooth. Traders once sold these teeth pretending they were unicorn horns, to be ground into powder and added to medicines.

• You can see a narwhal tooth in the *Mammals* exhibition at the Natural History Museum.

Dragon

• So-called "dragons' teeth" are still sold in China today, but they are usually the fossilised remains of extinct mammals such as the sabre-toothed cat and the three-toed horse.

• The next Chinese Year of the Dragon will be 2012. Colourful dragon costumes are worn during the Chinese New Year celebrations.

• St George, the legendary dragon-slayer, is the patron saint of England, Lebanon, Canada, Palestine and many other places. He is celebrated on 23rd April.

• The word "dinosaur" was invented by Richard Owen, the first head of the Natural History Museum, in 1842.

Phoenix

• The Phoenix is based on the Ancient Egyptian myth of the Benu bird, a heron-like form taken by the sun god Ra, which can re-create itself.

Yeti

• The distinguished mountaineer Sir Edmund Hillary and his Sherpa guide, Tenzing Norgay, came across giant footprints during their record ascent of Mount Everest in 1953.